GO FOR IT!

How I Stumbled into Success, Worked Hard, and Never Said No to Myself

A Memoir

by

Mary Overfelt

BookWorks
Overland Park, Kansas

Go For It! How I Stumbled into Success, Worked Hard, and Never Said No to Myself

ISBN: 0-9715655-0-3

Book cover and interior design by EAT Advertising and Design

Book publishing services by BookWorks Publishing, Marketing, Consulting

DEDICATION

This book is dedicated to my friend and mentor, Dr. James Helzberg, D.D.S., for encouraging me to enter the field of real estate.

ACKNOWLEDGMENTS

To my husband, Charles, and my children, Rocky and Leslie, for their loving support and confidence, which allowed me to pursue my dreams.

To my mother, Sarah Virginia Tauber Schweitzer, who always saw the sunny side of life with a great sense of humor.

To my father, Reverend Frank Herman Schweitzer, who set an example of strong beliefs and values.

To my grandmother, Mary Irene Schweitzer, who was my inspiration and namesake.

Finally, a very special thanks to my many loyal clients who made this story possible.

TABLE OF CONTENTS

PREFACE

In the years immediately following World War II, a woman's place was in the home. After the horrors of war, home and family reigned supreme. A housing boom began as returning GIs and their growing families needed decent housing. And soon manufacturers turned their attention to the production of appliances and other conveniences for the home. Women who had held the nation together during the war years, and discovered new strengths in the workplace, were once again back in the home, having babies and enjoying the new prosperity of the era.

This is the story of a woman of the 1950s, a housewife and mother who began what turned out to be an impressive and successful career with no long-range goals in mind. My story is told with a lot of love and humor. The experiences molded me into a successful real-estate developer, in a field dominated by men at the time.

I stumbled into a real-estate career rather haphazardly at the urging of a friend. But soon my creative ability and adventurous spirit found their expression, making me the person I am today ... one of Kansas City's best-known real-estate and land developers.

Almost from the beginning I was at the forefront with my ideas and innovations. In the 1970s, when America's women were burning their bras, donning pinstripes, and reading books on women's liberation, I was already a successful real-estate developer. To "find myself" and be successful I did not have to divorce a sexist husband – and I wore a pinstriped suit only because it was fashionable. I truly was a woman who had it all – a loving family, a supportive husband and friends, and a dynamic career.

You might ask, "Where's the story in this?" The point is that opportunities are always there. I had the option of just living the life of a woman married to a successful businessman. I didn't have to do anything spectacular with my life. I could have hidden in the shadows of my duties to my family. But at a time when stepping out on one's own was not encouraged for women, I took a dare.

I learned at an early age that I had the ability to sell – to earn money and pay for the things I wanted. The brass ring is always there. No matter where we are in life, we can grab it. Opportunities abound; we just have to have the curiosity and the belief in ourselves to make something of them.

From the start I had that uncompromising belief that I could learn to do anything that interested me. Coupled with a great sense of humor, a positive attitude and acknowledgment of my inherent gifts, this moved me forward. I am not one to either brag or whimper about the woes of my early years. There's very little *Sturm* and *Drang* in my story. Yet readers will undoubtedly find that my memoirs are both entertaining and encouraging. And as a secondary benefit, they might just learn to love their realtor!

AT THE BEGINNING

It was exactly eight o'clock in the morning when I walked into my office at the Loch Lloyd Country Club. As director of the club's real-estate development, I worked long hours, and enjoyed every moment of my days. I swept briskly past my cherry wood desk, and dropped my briefcase on a blue pin-striped chair near the bay window overlooking the lush green of the eighteenth fairway. Before sitting down I closed my eyes and took a deep breath. This was going to be a long day. But then, most days were long in the real-estate business.

Dressed in a gray wool suit, my chin-length brown hair curling slightly inwards, I felt I looked every bit the professional. I sat down at my desk resolutely and took another breath.

"Good morning," greeted my assistant, Sylvia Hanks, as she glided into the room, dropping a stack of pink message slips onto my desk. "That should keep you busy for a while," she murmured on her way out. I smiled as I thanked her, feeling lucky to have her work for me. Sylvia was not only very efficient, but also very affable and fun to work with.

"Say, Sylvia, you seem to be in a particularly good mood this morning. What's up?"

Sylvia beamed. "Oh, Mary, I was going to wait until you'd

had a chance to get settled before saying anything, but now that you've asked, Ted proposed this weekend."

I stood up and threw my arms around her. "I'm so happy for you, congratulations! When's the wedding?"

"Some time in July."

At that moment, our conversation was interrupted by the ring of the telephone.

Rushing to answer, "The call is for you, Mary," Sylvia announcd from her reception desk. "It's your friend Barbara."

My eyebrows rose as I picked up the phone. Why would Barbara be calling so early in the morning?

"Barbara, good morning," I said cheerfully as I picked up the phone.

"Good morning," Barbara said in a flat voice. I knew instantly that something was wrong.

"Barbara, what's wrong?"

"Oh, Mary, I hate to tell you this, but I'm afraid I have some very sad news. I just got word that Dr. Helzberg and his wife were killed in a car accident last night. I knew you would want to know."

I gasped and slumped down in my chair, placing my hand over my mouth and whispering numbly as tears ran down my cheek.

"What happened?"

"They were driving back from St. Louis on Interstate 70, when a car in the opposite lane jumped the median and landed on top of their car. They were killed instantly."

I started to cry softly. "Oh, Barbara, this is a terrible shock. Let me call you back. Thanks, thanks for calling." As I slowly replaced the receiver and slumped farther into my chair, I buried my face in my hands and started sobbing.

"Mary, what is it?" Sylvia was standing in my doorway, her forehead wrinkled in concern.

I dabbed my eyes with a tissue, then took a deep breath. "Barbara called to tell me that Dr. Helzberg, my dentist and friend, and his wife were killed in a car accident."

Sylvia rushed over and placed her arm on my shoulder. "I'm so sorry, Mary," she said awkwardly.

I sat up and forced a smile through my tears. "Thank you. I'm sorry for going on like this, but Dr. Helzberg was a very special person. He was not only a very good dentist, but he is actually the reason I got into the real-estate business."

With a perplexed look Sylvia blurted out, "Heavens, how did your dentist ever get you into real estate?"

"Years ago, I had to make a number of visits to Dr. Helzberg to correct my bite. At the time, my husband and I were building our first home, and so was Dr. Helzberg. Naturally, it was a prime subject during my many visits.

"We were on a shoestring budget. Our builder wasn't very experienced, but his bid fit our budget. Consequently, I kept a close check on everything. Since Charles was busy at the office, all the checking fell in my lap. I did my homework. I checked roofing materials, floor samples, wood, tiles, plumbing fixtures, doors, windows, appliances – you name it. I even acquired books on how to build homes!

"From the start I was not very impressed with the man who was hired to construct our brick fireplace, so I purchased a book on how to build fireplaces, and I studied it thoroughly. The day he built the fireplace, I sat by his side on a keg of nails, watching every move he made. Thank God he was a very pleasant person and didn't object to my being there watching. He did a good job, but he wasn't very neat or careful, so I had to keep reminding him to use his level. When he was nearly finished with the brick wall, I was sure he had gotten the hang of using the level so, since I was hungry, I decided to go to lunch. When I returned a little while later, he had left. It was easy to tell when I had gone to lunch, as there were a few bricks slightly out of line – something I learned to live with, and that no one else noticed.

"I'm sure our builder thought I got too involved in the building process, but not Dr. Helzberg. As a matter of fact, he was so impressed by my enthusiasm that he thought I would be excellent at real estate and wanted to introduce me to his father-in-law, Ben Fuller, who owned a real-estate company. Flattered, I accepted his offer, but I was really only being polite. I was thirty-five years old, a mother of two young children, and I was not looking for more to do.

"I remember the day I went for that interview forty-seven years ago. It seems as if it were only yesterday. The weather was much like today, a warm spring afternoon. It's strange that such a day could be so clear in my mind. I remember every detail.

"I was driving down Ward Parkway to meet Mr. Fuller, trying to figure out how to graciously decline the job offer I knew I was about to get, when I saw the most spectacular dogwood tree in full bloom in somebody's front yard. I slowed down to take another glimpse of those beautiful pink blossoms, almost causing an accident in the process. The alert driver behind me saved the day by readily applying his brakes. He backed up and quickly darted by me, giving me a killer look. I paused and thanked God for preventing the accident, and then proceeded down Ward Parkway.

"As I pulled into the parking space in front of the Prime Real Estate Company, east of 75th Street, my mind was set once again on a polite refusal of anything that even resembled a job offer. I began again to wonder why I had consented to the appointment in the first place. I had no intention of becoming a real-estate agent. Before leaving the car, I took a few moments to collect my thoughts.

"A number of ways to politely refuse the job went through my mind: 'Thank you for your kind offer, but it really doesn't suit me right now.' 'I'm flattered that you think I could sell real estate, but I'm really too busy.'

"Then I straightened my navy blue linen dress, glanced up at the Prime Real Estate Properties sign, and slowly opened the door. The receptionist greeted me with a friendly smile.

"Hello, my name is Mary Overfelt. I'm here to see Mr. Fuller."

"Of course, Mrs. Overfelt. Mr. Fuller is expecting you. I'll let him know you're here. You shouldn't have to wait long. Won't you have a seat?"

"I glanced around the reception room. Real-estate agents were busily entering and exiting. There were people of all ages – male and female. In the very next moment, I had a complete change of heart about selling real estate.

"A young woman, not much older than myself, appeared from one of the offices. As she walked toward the door, the receptionist stopped her. "Your check is ready from your recent sale," she said jovially. "Don't spend that two thousand dollars all in one place."

"TWO THOUSAND DOLLARS!" I was impressed!

"Before the young woman left the office, I sneaked another glance at her. Her brown hair was tied up in a smart little bun and she was wearing just enough makeup to draw attention to her handsome features. Her suit was nicely tailored and she looked very professional.

"Then it struck me. If she could make two thousand dollars by selling one house, so could I. I began to think of what I could do with the extra money: buy furniture for our new house, little extras for the children. Two thousand dollars then was more like ten thousand now.

"I even thought maybe I could earn enough to go to the Oberammergau passion play in Germany. I had heard a lecture on it from my English teacher back in high school. She presented such a vivid picture of the play that I promised myself that some day, before I was forty, I would see that play. When you're that young, you think you'd be over the hill by forty."

"I've never heard of it," said Sylvia in a curious tone. "It must be wonderful. Tell me about it."

"Oberammergau is a quaint little village in the foothills of the Bavarian Alps in Germany famous for the performance of the passion play, which normally is presented every ten years. The pageantry portrays the life and death of Jesus. In the sixteenth century, as the black plague swept through the village, killing many people, the villagers promised God that if he would lift the plague from their village, they would perform the passion play every ten years. God lifted the plague and they have kept to their promise every since."

"Tell me, did you ever see the play?"

With a smile, I responded, "As a matter of fact, I celebrated my fortieth birthday in Oberammergau."

"Wow! You surely get what you go after, Mary."

"While I was dreaming of what I could do with two thousand dollars, the next thing I knew a gray-haired gentleman was standing in front of me saying my name and politely extending his hand. To tell you the truth, my plans to reject Mr. Fuller's potential offer were fading fast as I shook his hand and followed him to his office. Not more than a half hour later, I emerged, the newest member of the Fuller Real Estate Company.

"And that's about it. I've been in the business ever since."

"What a great story," Sylvia said. "Dr. Helzberg sure knew what he was doing when he suggested you go into real estate."

"He sure did."

"So, how did you become a developer and a builder?"

"Oh, that's a long story. I'll tell you about that some other time. I have too much work to do now."

The following Wednesday morning, I arrived in my office at seven fifteen to catch up on paperwork before heading to the memorial service for Dr. Helzberg and his wife. Driving down Ward Parkway, my eyes fell on the same dogwood tree I had noticed forty-seven years ago on my way to meet Mr. Fuller. Again the tree was in full bloom. Even though it was old and showed signs of many trimmings, it was still beautiful. The tree made me realize how long I had been in the real-estate business. I quickly glanced at the sky and thanked God for giving me strength and enthusiasm to continue working and enjoying the many blessings of life.

As I sat quietly in the synagogue paying my last respects to

Dr. Helzberg, the man who had the sense to identify and encourage my talent as a realtor, my mind drifted back in time. Vivid pictures began dancing through my head. For that brief moment, I felt as if I was able to see my entire life playing out in my mind.

After that appointment with Mr. Fuller, I took the necessary tests to get my real-estate licenses both in Missouri and Kansas. At my first sales meeting, Mr. Fuller introduced me to the other agents and assigned me a desk next to Melva's. Melva had a cigarette voice, a thick, middle-aged waist, and hair that was brittle from many dye jobs. As soon as I sat down, Melva volunteered to fill me in on the office gossip. She was very bitter, nosy, and gossipy. I cringed as she began filling me in.

"See that woman over there, the one with the gray hair?" Melva asked. "That's Dr. Oliver's widow. She really doesn't have to work, as her husband was well off. People like her shouldn't work because it takes sales away from people like me who really need the money.

"See that man who just came in?" she continued. "That's Mr. Porter. I can't stand him. He's a retired football coach, thinks he's God's gift to women. The only reason he sells a lot of real estate is that he has a lot of contacts."

It didn't take me long to realize that Melva was one very unhappy camper. However, I did feel sorry for her after she revealed that her husband had died very suddenly with no insurance, leaving her with two small children to raise by herself.

While Melva was acquainting me with the woes of the office, I noticed the girl across the aisle grinning at me. When I caught her eye, she winked ever so slightly. She appeared to be the opposite of Melva. When she soon walked over to introduce herself, I breathed a sigh of relief at having Melva's litany of criticism interrupted.

"Hi, I'm Luann. Welcome on board. If I can help you at any time, please let me know." Luann's sunny disposition and positive attitude made my day.

I organized my desk and then decided to go home to my children. As I was leaving, Mr. Fuller darted from his office to remind me that he was pleased to have me on board and assured me that I would do well in real estate.

On my way home, I picked up the children at Grandmother Overfelt's, who lived within blocks of our house. At dinner that night, Charles listened attentively to my description of my first day at the office. Charles was my best supporter. He knew I would be excellent at anything I put my mind to, especially real estate, since he had seen me design our first home and watch the construction from start to finish.

It was hard to go to sleep that night. Despite all the excitement, I wasn't sure I really wanted to be a real-estate agent, or if I had the time. But, then, it could be the one way to earn enough money to go to Oberammergau. With two young children, a new home that needed a lot, and a husband who had just started his own business, I couldn't imagine our budget ballooning enough to afford such a trip. Yes!

THE FIRST LESSON I LEARNED IN REAL ESTATE IS TO SET GOALS. I WOULD TRY IT AT LEAST UNTIL I HAD EARNED ENOUGH MONEY FOR MY DREAM TRIP.

SCOTCH AND ROSES

I was standing one afternoon at the kitchen sink cleaning up the mess I had made while baking the children's favorite cookies. Rocky was off to school and Leslie was taking her afternoon nap. The telephone rang and I ran to get it so as not to wake Leslie. It was my brother, Paul, calling from Toledo.

"Paul, great to hear from you, how's everyone?"

"Mary, I have a customer for you," said Paul, getting right to the point. "We're transferring Mr. Brown to Kansas City, where he will be the district manager. I have already spoken to our executive secretary in Kansas City about you and she is expecting your call."

As he gave me the secretary's name and number, Paul was very emphatic that I call her immediately.

"Thanks for thinking of me."

"Well, you told me last month that you got your real-estate license, so naturally I thought of you."

As usual, I jumped at the opportunity immediately and called Jane, the secretary. She was very pleasant and very precise as she dictated the Browns' schedule and requisites.

"Mrs. Brown does not drive, so it will be necessary to find a home within walking distance of shopping areas. Her furniture is very traditional. She's an enthusiastic gardener. They have no children."

The list seemed endless. By the time I finished talking to Jane, I felt I knew Mrs. Brown personally.

"The Browns will be in Kansas City next Monday," continued Jane. "The plans are that Mrs. Brown will look at homes all day Monday and Tuesday while her husband is in meetings. On Wednesday, Mr. Brown will join his wife to review the homes she has selected.

"Now," Jane went on, "I have arranged for a J. C. Nichols agent to show Mrs. Brown homes on Monday, so I'll have you take Mrs. Brown out on Tuesday."

Even though I was new in the business, I knew that J. C. Nichols was one of the largest real-estate companies in Kansas City. I was also well aware that my chance of selling a home to the Browns was slim if I followed a J. C. Nichols agent.

"Would it be possible for me to show Mrs. Brown homes on Monday and let J. C. Nichols work with her on Tuesday?" I quickly asked.

Not suspecting my motives, Jane replied, "I see no problem with that. You can pick Mrs. Brown up Monday morning at nine at the Muehlebach Hotel downtown. I'll have J.C. Nichols take her out on Tuesday."

I thanked Jane, and as I put the receiver back in its place, I thanked God for my first customer.

Immediately, I called Grandmother Overfelt to see if she would be available to take care of the children for a few days. As usual, she was delighted – Grandmother's whole life was centered around her family. As soon as she arrived the next morning, I headed to the office. Melva was on board duty that morning, which meant that she sat at the front desk and answered the telephone and helped anyone who walked in. She immediately wanted to know why I was checking all the listing sheets.

"I'm so excited. I have my first client," I answered.

"Well, how did you get a customer?" she asked. "Did Mr. Fuller give you the lead? He never gives me one."

"No, Melva, my brother in Toledo gave me the client."

After I checked all of the listings that might fit the Browns' needs, I decided to check the area for other company listings.

Things were different in 1955. Multiple-listing services did not exist. There were no computers. You basically had to check signs in yards to be sure you didn't miss a listing.

After checking around, I found the one area that would be perfect for the Browns. The problem was that it was a J. C. Nichols development and all the homes on the market there had J. C. Nichols signs in the yards. In those days, when you co-opped with J. C. Nichols, you had to register your client's name. Knowing they had the Brown's name registered, I could not co-op with them. But I wasn't giving up that easily. I decided to knock on doors in the neighborhood and do my own homework.

Maybe someone was about to put their home on the market or maybe I could talk someone into selling their home. I knocked on eight doors. Either no one was home or they didn't want to sell. Just as I was about to go home, I decided to try one more house. The lady who opened the door was very pleasant, but said she wasn't selling her home. However, she informed me that she had heard that Dr. Thomas down the street was thinking about selling. She pointed to the home. I thanked her for the tip and headed straight to the Thomas' home.

Mrs. Thomas, a very attractive woman with dark hair pulled back in a low bun, answered the door. I showed her my card as I introduced myself. Then I quickly stated that I had heard they might be selling their home and that I had a top executive and his wife coming to town for whom I thought the area would be perfect.

In a very soft, dignified voice, Mrs. Thomas said, "Darling, come back next week." As I turned to leave, I heard a voice from inside say, "Dear, let her in." Mrs. Thomas, in a very recoiled manner, ushered me into the library where the doctor greeted me as his wife promptly disappeared.

Dr. Thomas was a very charming elderly man. He was having his afternoon scotch and invited me to join him.

"Do you like Scotch? This is a very special imported brand."

"Yes, I would be delighted to join you, Dr. Thomas." I thought scotch tasted like medicine, but I would be happy to have a scotch if it would help get me the listing.

After pouring me a drink, Dr. Thomas proceeded to ask me about my client. I informed him that my clients were a well-qualified executive and his wife and that the location would be ideal for their wants. He then took me on a tour of the home. It was a beautiful home in A-one condition. Their furniture was very traditional. I fell in love with the home immediately. Best of all, the price was within the Browns' budget.

Dr. Thomas was a gardener (how perfect, considering Mrs. Brown's hobby), and especially proud of his roses, which he insisted on showing me. I was still nursing my drink, and as I viewed the rose garden, I surreptitiously emptied my glass in the garden. As we returned to the library, the doctor noticed that my glass was empty and graciously offered me another drink.

"Best if I don't have another drink since I'm driving," I quickly responded.

"Mary, I want to be honest with you," said Dr. Thomas. "I promised J. C. Nichols that they could list this home on Monday at noon."

"Please give me until Monday at one o'clock," I begged. "If my clients don't like the home, you can give it to J. C. Nichols. But I just know they are going to want your beautiful home. Besides, there will be no contingencies on financing as they are well qualified."

"Fair enough. You have my word," replied Dr. Thomas, extending his hand to seal his words with a firm handshake.

As I drove home, I breathed a sigh of relief and thanked God for helping me. Since my father was a minister, thanking God was something instilled in me from childhood.

I met Mrs. Brown Monday morning as planned. After showing her several homes that she wasn't too excited about, I promised her that she would fall in love with the next one. As we pulled up in front of the Thomas' home, Mrs. Brown exclaimed, "Oh my, I see what you mean."

When she stepped into the front entry, I heard a sigh of pleasure. Even the carpet was the right color for their furniture. After seeing the rest of the inside, Mrs. Brown was sure that this home would soon be theirs.

The next step was to figure out how to get Mr. Brown out of a meeting to approve the home. I told Mrs. Brown that if she really wanted the home, she would have to get her husband's approval before one o'clock, as the home was then going to be listed exclusively with another company.

"You were right," she said. "The home is perfect for us. May I use the phone to call Dick? I know he'll like it."

I ushered her into the library to use the phone. After getting her husband out of a meeting, she explained the urgency to him. She made it clear that she had found the perfect home for them and that he had to come and see it immediately or they would lose it to another company.

Mr. Brown's secretary immediately chauffeured him to the house. As he stepped from the car, it was obvious that he was not in a very receptive mood. "What did you do, let her sell you the first home she showed you?" he asked brusquely.

"Now, Dick," replied his wife, "Don't get upset until you see it. It is perfect for us."

Mr. Brown turned to me with a curt introduction. He then kept a very stern face and said nothing as I showed him the house. Finally, he broke the silence and said, "This is a very lovely home. If I have to sign a contract before one o'clock, Mary, I need someone here to appraise it immediately."

I excused myself and went to the library to call Mr. Fuller.

"Could you help me? I found a home in Fairway and have a buyer for it if I can get it appraised right now. The address is 5525 Fairway. No. It isn't a J. C. Nichols listing. It's my listing until one o'clock."

Mr. Fuller sounded confused, wondering how I – totally new in the business – had not only gotten a listing in Fairway but had a customer for it already. "Mr. Fuller," I continued, "my customer is a top executive. Would you stay and write the long form contract, since I don't want to make any mistakes? I'll explain everything later."

While waiting for Mr. Fuller to arrive, the Browns enjoyed Dr. Thomas' beautiful rose garden. When Mr. Fuller arrived, I introduced him as the appraiser. Mr. Fuller was a very dignified gentleman, who seemed to impress Mr. Brown. After checking the home from the basement up, Mr. Fuller assured the Browns that the asking price was fair, considering the condition of the home and the location.

Mr. Brown soon called me aside, "Get rid of the appraiser and let's write the contract."

"Mr. Fuller is my broker; he will write the contract."

"You mean you called your broker to appraise the home? Naturally, he would agree with the price."

Up until now, Mr. Brown had intimidated me. I realized that it was time to speak up.

"I want you to know that Mr. Fuller is a very honorable man. He knows this area better than any banker or appraiser. I've shown your wife several other homes in the same price range and I'm sure she'll be the first to agree that they don't begin to compare to this home or this area."

"Okay, then," said Mr. Brown, "let's get the contract written up."

Mr. Fuller handled Mr. Brown very tactfully and quickly, but carefully, and wrote the contract, which the Browns signed immediately. As Mr. Fuller left, I thanked him and said I would be in the office in the morning.

I invited the Browns to join Charles and me for dinner that night, which they gratefully accepted.

As for the Thomases, they were pleased that they received their asking price so quickly. When the deal closed, I sent the doctor a bottle of his favorite scotch.

My spirits were high. I not only found the perfect home for the Browns, but also won a sale from the biggest real-estate company. When I told Mr. Fuller how I had gotten the listing, he was surprised and praised me highly.

THE SECOND LESSON I LEARNED IN REAL ESTATE WAS TO "GO FOR IT!" AND DON'T GET DISCOURAGED.

P. S. The Browns lived in the home until Mr. Brown retired and they moved to Florida. They never forgot me, even after leaving the area. For years I continued to receive Christmas cards inquiring about me and my family.

MY FIRST OPEN HOUSE

Within a week of my first day at work, Mr. Fuller called me into his office. "Mary, I have a house I'd like for you to hold open next Sunday."

"I'd be happy to," I replied.

"Here's a listing sheet. You need to preview the home and familiarize yourself with the details on this sheet. You will need to know about the taxes, the lot size, utility bills and other particulars without having to look those items up if you are asked by a potential buyer." I nodded appreciatively as Mr. Fuller continued to explain the procedures for open houses.

I left Mr. Fuller's office with a confident smile and immediately went back to my desk. It was clear that Melva was curious to know what Mr. Fuller had been discussing with me. Before she could say anything, I shared the good news with her.

"Melva, guess what? Mr. Fuller gave me a listing to work and I'm going to have my first open house this Sunday!"

She rolled her eyes dramatically, then said, "I told you he catered to the young girls. What house is it?"

When I told her the address, Melva began to laugh. "What's so funny?" I asked. "It's a dog of a house. It's been on the market forever, atrocious decor, and needs tons of work."

"Oh, I don't know. It doesn't look that bad to me," I said, glancing at a picture of a two-story English Tudor on the listing.

"Trust me, it's bad. You'll be lucky if you have a single looker on Sunday."

After making an appointment with the owners, I drove out to preview the home dreading that Melva was right.

But when I pulled into the driveway, I smiled to myself. Although the shrubbery was overgrown, the exterior wood trim was in dire need of a paint job, and some storm windows were missing, the house was quite charming. The flagstone pathway leading up to the arched doorway did need some repair, but I could see that with a little work, it could be a lovely home.

"Mary?" asked the gray-haired man who opened the door.

"Yes. You must be Mr. Nash." I shook his hand and was ushered into the living room. I maintained a stiff smile as I surveyed the surroundings: the outdated decor, the jumble of mismatched furniture and the assortment of plastic flower arrangements that seemed to be growing out of every nook and cranny.

Just then, a small gray-haired woman with a friendly smile walked into the room and introduced herself as Mrs. Nash. "Now," she said sweetly, "Why don't I show you the rest of our house? I'm sure you've heard that we've had a slightly difficult time selling it. I want to give it to another company, but Mr. Nash won't. He's an old friend of Mr. Fuller's brother. I hope you can sell it. We have found a place in the Ozarks that we want to buy, if we could only get this place sold."

I smiled nervously. "Tell me, Mrs. Nash, just how many salespeople has Mr. Fuller put on this home?"

"Oh, four or five. I forget," she replied.

Mrs. Nash then led me into the small, drab kitchen. The avocado green refrigerator matched the counter tops, the orange linoleum floor looked as if it hadn't been replaced in decades, and the dark orange walls made me feel slightly claustrophobic.

I took a deep breath and followed Mrs. Nash upstairs. When

I saw the plastic flower arrangement in the bidet, I burst out laughing. Mrs. Nash laughed too. "You know, Mary, we never use that – it is perfect for some flowers."

Standing at the front door at the end of the tour, I tried to suppress my discouragement. "So, what do you think?" asked Mr. Nash, as I prepared to leave. "Can you sell it?"

"I'll sure do my best. Thank you for the tour. I'll plan to have an open house this Sunday from one o'clock to five."

As I climbed into my car, I had to admit that Melva might just be right.

But by the time Sunday rolled around, I had managed to turn my despair into hope. The architecture was good and the construction was good, the house just needed to be decorated with cheery colors and updated appliances, as well as new carpet and window treatments.

A few minutes after I arrived, the Nashes left. I reviewed the listing sheet again to be sure I was familiar with all the facts about the house. While waiting for people to arrive, I scanned the house. The floors were carpeted wall to wall. Could the floors possibly be hardwood? My curiosity got the best of me. I got a knife from the kitchen and carefully pried up a small corner of the carpet in the living room. It was hardwood! I checked the dining room – it was hardwood too. After making sure the corners of the carpet were properly tucked back in place again, my enthusiasm grew. What a terrific selling point! I thought the price was too high because of all the work that had to be done. I could handle that. I had been selling all of my life and knew that the right price was the answer.

When I was ten years old, I wanted a pair of ball-bearing roller skates. It was during the Depression and my father could only afford the less expensive skates since he had three pairs to buy for my brother, sister and me. The inexpensive ones were $1.95, the ball-bearing ones were $2.95. Already then, I didn't give up very easily. Yo-yos were the rage at the time. When your yo-yo string broke, two cents would buy a new one at the store.

Instead of spending money on new strings, I replaced mine by using a piece from my mother's ball of string and covering it with bee's wax from my father's fishing basket, which gave it the same strength as the purchased ones. Why not make them to sell? If the store sold them for two cents, I would undersell the store by one penny. I made and sold enough strings to purchase my own ball-bearing skates.

I knew I would have to talk Mr. and Mrs. Nash into reducing the price of their home in order to be able to sell it. I would worry about that when I got an interested buyer. Two hours had passed and no one came. Several people drove by, stopped to look, but drove on. At five o'clock, Mr. and Mrs. Nash had not returned, so I locked up and left – discouraged.

The next Sunday, I took a good book to read during the open house. I had been reading for two hours when the door bell suddenly rang. I jumped up and opened the door to a middle-aged couple. “Welcome,” I said, smiling and gesturing toward the living room. The woman took a quick glance around and before I could say a word, she turned to her husband and ushered him out saying, “Harold, this isn't our house.”

I sighed heavily as I closed the door behind them. “There's got to be a way of making this place look better,” I thought to myself. Glancing around the room, I rearranged several chairs to make the room look larger. “I wonder if this would make a difference,” I said out loud, as I removed one of the plastic flower arrangements from the coffee table. I raised my eyebrows and nodded. Then I quickly collected all the other plastic flower arrangements scattered thoughout the first floor and stashed them on the back porch. Yes! The place already looked better. I was glad the Nashes had gone to the lake for the weekend and wouldn't be back until later in the evening. I would have ample time to return the flowers and furniture as they were originally before leaving for the day.

Satisfied with my work, I sat down on an overstuffed chair,

pulled out the daily newspaper from my briefcase and relaxed for the next three hours.

It was four thirty. In thirty minutes the open house was scheduled to close and not another person had showed. I headed for the porch to gather up the plastic flowers when I heard a car pulling into the driveway. Quickly, I returned to the living room to greet a young couple.

"Hello," I said casually, as the couple walked in.

"I'm Carol Turner and this is my husband, Jack."

"It's nice to meet you."

As the couple lingered in the living room, I tried to explain that the room was larger than it appeared because of all the furniture. Carol assured me that the size was perfect for them.

Jack spoke up immediately, "How much is this home?"

I told them the price and asked if it was in their price bracket. "That depends on how much work has to be done," Jack replied. I quickly added, "You should know that the floors under the carpet are all hardwood, which is a great plus." Both were pleased to hear that.

I agreed with Jack that there was a lot of work to be done and noted that I knew some good workmen if he needed them. Jack smiled and thanked me.

I proceeded to escort the couple through the rest of the home. Jack headed for the basement while I showed Carol the kitchen. Barely taking one look, Carol said, "This will never do. It's too small." I immediately suggested that they could knock out the wall between the kitchen and dinette to make a country kitchen. That idea made Carol's ears perk up. "Could that be done?"

I replied that I was quite sure that the wall was not a bearing wall and that it could be done. Carol called Jack from the basement. "Jack, Mary suggested that we could remove the wall to the dinette and make a country kitchen. Wouldn't that be great?" At this point, Carol was starting to sell Jack. Jack agreed that it could be done. He then announced that the basement was in good condition, but the furnace would have to be checked. I assured him that the owners would have that done.

Jack then wanted to sit down and talk about the price. "What do you think the owners will take for this house?" I threw the question back in Jack's lap. "What do you think would be fair to offer?" Jack thought for a few minutes and came back with a price that was $10,000 less than the asking price. "Let me write it up for that and we'll see what happens," I said calmly.

I proceeded to write up a short form, which both Jack and Carol signed. They also gave me a check for $2,000 made out to Fuller Real Estate Company. I told Jack I would present the offer as soon as the owners returned from the lake and I would get back to them at once. The couple was happy, and as they left, Carol turned to me and said, "I do hope they accept our offer because we could make this such a beautiful home." I smiled and reassured her that I would do my best.

The Turners had no more pulled out of the driveway when the Nashes pulled in.

"Well," Mr. Nash asked cautiously, "how did it go?"

"Very well. We got an offer."

"What?" he blurted out, his eyes wide open. "Helen, did you hear that?"

Her lips pursed, Helen nodded stiffly as she surveyed the room. I followed her gaze and soon realized that she was looking for her plastic flower arrangements. "Oh, my goodness," I said, smacking my palm against my forehead. "I forgot the flowers, Mrs. Nash. I'm so sorry! I put them on the back porch."

Mrs. Nash's jaw was set in anger, but before she had a chance to utter a word, her husband broke in, "The hell with the flowers! I never liked all that junk anyhow. Where's the contract and how much did they offer?"

Handing him the signed contract, I said, almost apologetically, "The Turners felt this was a reasonable offer. Now, I know it's ten thousand less than your asking price, but they felt that ..."

"We'll take it," Mr. Nash interjected, grabbing the contract enthusiastically. "We never expected to get our asking price anyway. This house needs everything. Where's the pen and where do we sign? Now, we can go ahead with our lake house." Before leaving I helped Mrs. Nash replace her flowers.

Monday morning at our sales meeting, Mr. Fuller congratulated me on the sale. Melva was shocked as she leaned over to me and said, "You actually sold that house?"

"Yes," I smiled triumphantly, "I sold it, that dog of a house."

THIS SCENARIO PROVES THE AGE-OLD SAYING THAT IF THE PRICE IS RIGHT THERE'S A BUYER FOR EVERY HOME.

SELLING THE MOTEL

Looking back after forty-seven years in the real-estate business, I realize that Lady Luck had been on my side. Only six months after I had received my license, one evening during dinner Charles said, "Incidentally, dear, would you like to sell a motel in Kirksville?" Kirksville, Charles' hometown, is about 156 miles from Kansas City.

I was in shock and flattered to think that my husband thought I was capable of handling a sale of that magnitude. Charles explained that he heard of the potential sale of the motel from a client, adding that if I wanted the listing, he was sure he could get it for me.

I smiled and said, "Dear, it's so sweet of you to think of me, but let's face it, I'm not experienced enough to handle a motel. I'm not comfortable about writing a contract on a house, let alone a complicated contract to consummate a motel sale."

But as I was doing the dishes later that evening, my thoughts reverted to the motel. What a commission that would be! I could go to the Oberammergau play and buy things we needed, like a dishwasher. In fact, I had already planned a spot in the kitchen counter for it, when we could afford it. Yes! I'll take that listing and figure a way to handle it, I decided. I rushed into the living room where Charles was reading the evening paper and told him I had changed my mind. I would take the listing after all. Charles smiled, knowing full well I could not turn down a challenge.

Charles arranged for me to call Mrs. Conroy, the owner of the motel, who was recently widowed and didn't want the responsibility of running the place. I was very apprehensive about calling the lady, knowing she would ask me about my experience in selling motels. I couldn't admit that I had been in the business for only six months. How should I handle it? I decided I would immediately emphasize the large company I worked for, both in residential and commercial real estate. Surprisingly, when I called Mrs. Conroy, she didn't question me about my experience but thanked me for calling. She was most anxious to show me the motel, so I wasted no time in setting up an appointment.

I immediately called Mr. Fuller about the listing I was about to get. He was impressed by my ambition and began to realize he had hired a very aspiring agent. He also could see the dollars for the company.

It was August and the temperature was soaring into the 90s. I dreaded the drive to Kirksville as my car wasn't air-conditioned. Driving out of town I decided to stop at the Ford dealership where Charles had bought our cars to see if I could rent an air-conditioned car. The dealer was accommodating and I soon drove off in cool comfort.

I had no trouble finding the motel. As soon as I met Mrs. Conroy, I knew we would be friends. Mrs. Conroy was very benevolent and made me feel comfortable about pursuing the listing agreement. After touring the motel, reviewing the guest rooms, dining room and grounds, I accompanied Mrs. Conroy to the office. She had all the necessary paperwork ready and was very thorough about explaining the entire operation of the motel.

By this time, Mrs. Conroy insisted that I call her Joan. She signed the exclusive contract to sell the motel, fully confident that I knew what I was doing. Driving home that evening, I realized what a huge responsibility I had accepted.

The next day I hurried to the office to present the listing to Mr. Fuller, who was amazed and dumbfounded. He was even more surprised, but also proud of me, when I asked if I could advertise the motel in the *Wall Street Journal*. But he agreed and proceeded to help me write the ad.

For several weeks we got no response to the ad. Then one day while I was at home, I received a call from the office with instructions to call a Mr. White in Cincinnati. After asking me many questions pertaining to the motel, Mr. White said he would like to meet me in Kirksville and see it. I arranged a meeting for the following week. The meeting went well. Mr. White spent most of his time with Joan going over the books and I felt like a fifth wheel.

Mr. White was very quiet, pleasant, but hard to read. When he left, he said he would think about it and get back to me. Joan complimented me on producing a prospect so quickly. I thanked her and promised to keep her informed.

I reported the meeting with Mr. White to Mr. Fuller, who was pleased and encouraged me to keep advertising. Melva and other co-workers became very inquisitive about my listing in Kirksville, insinuating that Mr. Fuller must have given me the listing. I expected the remarks from Melva, but not from the other co-workers and quickly straightened them out on the subject.

Two weeks went by and I still hadn't heard from Mr. White. I finally decided to call him and was disappointed when his secretary informed me that he was in Europe and wouldn't be back for two weeks. I left my name and number and asked that he call me upon his return.

Several weeks later, I was pleasantly surprised to receive a call from Mr. White, who started out by apologizing for not having called earlier. He was still interested in the motel and wanted to meet again in Kirksville to discuss several options relative to purchasing the motel. We promptly set a date that would be convenient for him. After confirming the date with Joan, I consulted with my broker. Mr. Fuller suggested that he go with me on this appointment and I heartily agreed. We all met in Kirksville, where Mr. Fuller took over masterfully. While he worked out the financing and contract details, I took inventory. The transaction went smoothly – Joan was happy, I had a very satisfied client, and Mr. Fuller was a pleased broker.

Considering all that had to be done, it was late before we finished, so Joan insisted that everyone have dinner before starting home. Mr. White graciously declined, as he had to catch a flight, but after making calls home, Mr. Fuller and I stayed for dinner. During dinner, Joan casually mentioned that she was thinking of moving to Kansas City.

"You'll love Kansas City," I chimed in. "You can drive back with me and look at some homes."

"If it wouldn't be any trouble I would love to."

"No trouble at all. There are several motels near Leawood where I live, and you could stay in one of them," I replied. Joan, with a childlike excitement, said she was ready to pack.

Mr. Fuller was amazed at my ability to take control of a situation. I may not have known the financial end of real estate, but I had no inhibitions about making things happen.

Driving back to Kansas City that evening, I quizzed Joan on her criteria for a home. My mind began to turn. I would have to get up early in order to check for listings and set up appointments. I also thought of the charming English Tudor around the corner from my own home. The Fosters had mentioned that they were thinking of selling, but not until they had redecorated some rooms. Maybe I could talk them into letting me show the house after all.

I checked Joan into a hotel and promised to pick her up the next morning at nine o'clock for breakfast. I was exhausted by the time I got home, and was thankful that the children were at their grandmother's home. Charles was still up reading, and together we shared the excitement of the motel sale.

The next morning I was up at the crack of dawn checking listings and waiting for a decent hour to call Carol, my neighbor, to see if I could show their home. Being in the same neighborhood, I knew the price would be right for Joan. I also knew how charming Carol's home was, with well-groomed gardens.

Finally I called. "Carol, this is Mary. I hope I'm not calling too early. I have an out-of-town client who I think would love your home. There's no problem with financing, she has the cash, and occupancy could be arranged to suit you. Also, if my client should buy your home, you'll never have the hassle of putting it on the market and going through all the showings."

My plan sounded good to Carol, who promised she would check with her husband in the evening and let me know.

"But I'm picking up my client at the hotel in forty-five minutes. Call your husband at work right now. I have good vibes on this." Carol called me back shortly and agreed to the one-time showing.

I met Joan at the hotel and we had a leisurely breakfast, thereby giving Carol time to make the beds and get the house in order. I told Joan about the English Tudor home and how excited I was to show it to her. It was obvious that she was placing a lot of confidence in my judgment as to the right home and location. I was sure she would like the location and hoped she would like the home.

As soon as I pulled up in front of the home, Joan exclaimed, "Mary, I love it already."

"Now wait until you see the inside," I added. I was sure Joan would love that too. And she did. I not only showed her the home, but also drove around the neighborhood pointing out Leawood Country Club and the convenient shopping center nearby. Joan was ready to buy the house.

I immediately drove to my office to write the contract. Mr. Fuller was surprised to see me in the office so soon. When I told him I was there to write a contract on a home that wasn't even on the market, he was beginning to think I was some superwoman. I was too new in the business to realize I had pulled a real coup.

Within a year, Joan had met a man at the club and they were to be married. She asked me to be her maid of honor. I felt really good about helping Joan start her new life. What a beautiful ending!

IT WAS A GREAT SALE IN MANY WAYS. I LEARNED TO TAKE RISKS BY BROADENING MY PROSPECTS.

MY FIRST LISTING

It was a cold morning in January and I sat shivering inside my navy blue wool blazer. I was on board duty, which was not my favorite part of the job. But since each agent was required to take an occasional turn on board duty, I tolerated it as best I could.

"Fuller Real Estate Company," I said into the receiver for the fourteenth time that morning. "May I help you?"

"Yes, this is Donna Whitney. My husband and I would like to sell our home and a friend of ours recommended the Fuller Company."

I perked up and assured Mrs. Whitney that I would be happy to meet with them about selling their home.

Mrs. Whitney asked if it would be convenient for me to meet with her and her husband that evening at about seven o'clock.

"Certainly," I replied with my usual enthusiasm.

When Mrs. Whitney gave me her telephone number and address, I nearly gasped. It was in the old exclusive Country Club area of Kansas City. It would be a coup to get my sign up in that area.

My duty at the front desk was up at noon, and Luann was to take over for the afternoon. I couldn't wait to tell her about the listing I was hoping to get and also wanted to ask her for advice. Meanwhile, I started to look at the office files to see if I could find any sales in the area made by the company in the past year for comparisons .

Of course, Melva, who was hanging around the office that morning, wanted to know why I was checking the office files. I told her about Mrs. Whitney's call. She was quick to warn me that I did not have the experience to handle a home in that area and that I should hand it over to a more experienced agent, who would then give me a finder's fee. I ignored Melva's remark and continued checking the office files. Down deep in my heart I feared the meaning of Melva's remarks, but I was determined to get the listing after all.

When Luann came to relieve me, she suggested that I ask Mr. Fuller to have four or five top sales agents review the home with me to be sure we established a fair price.

After gathering the information I needed, I left the office and drove through the Whitneys' neighborhood, where I searched the yards for real-estate signs. I found two, both from Fuller's competitors. As soon as I arrived home that afternoon, I called the agents who were handling these listings to ask them about the homes' features and the listing prices.

Armed with a detailed profile of the neighborhood, I drove to the Whitneys' home later that evening, arriving promptly at seven o'clock.

Mr. Whitney, a tall middle-aged gentleman, greeted me at the front door and welcomed me into a spacious foyer. A sparkling chandelier graced the ceiling, and a walnut staircase curved gently upwards from the marbled floor.

"Hello, Mary," said a tall, thin woman with short, blonde hair and a broad smile. "I'm Donna Whitney. It's so good of you to come out on this cold night. May I take your coat and hat?"

Mr. and Mrs. Whitney immediately made me feel at home as they guided me through their home.

One hour later, I was sitting on a soft leather chair in front of a roaring fire in their enormous living room.

"Well, you certainly have a remarkable home," I said genuinely, getting a notebook out of my briefcase. "It's simply lovely. I'm convinced that we won't have any difficulty selling it."

"Now, since we spoke this morning, Mrs. Whitney, I've had a chance to do a little research on your neighborhood. It looks like the homes in this area are selling for between three and four hundred thousand dollars, and I would speculate that yours would be at the upper end of that scale. But I would feel more comfortable if I could have a few of my company's top salespeople come out and assess your home. If we pool our resources, I think we'll be able to come up with exactly the right price."

"Well, you certainly have done your homework, Mary," said Mr. Whitney. "I'm impressed. And I think you have a good idea. We'd be happy to have your colleagues come out to evaluate our home. You just name the time. The sooner, the better, because Donna and I are most anxious to start building a home in the new Leawood area."

"How about if I call you tomorrow to set up a time?" I promptly suggested.

"Perfect," Donna smiled.

"You know, I must say, I'm pleased to list such a beautiful home. It's quite unique in quality and workmanship."

"You're kind," said Donna, as the three of us stood up and began walking toward the foyer. "Thank you again for coming out on this cold winter night. We'll talk to you tomorrow."

As I drove home I felt very pleased with the meeting, but I couldn't understand why the Whitneys wanted to sell such a beautiful home. I would have given anything to own such a superb home in one of the best neighborhoods in the city.

The following day, I asked Mr. Fuller to select five of the top sales agents to evaluate the Whitney home and arranged for them to see the home that afternoon. After a careful review, they priced the home at $375,000, a price that pleased the sellers. (This home, in 2002, would sell for well over a million dollars.)

That evening, I quickly drafted an ad for the home to be advertised in the Sunday newspaper.

By noon on Sunday, I had received three calls on the ad and had already scheduled a showing for Monday afternoon. To my disappointment, Monday turned out to be a very cold and snowy day. Thick clouds blocked out the sun and the wind was chilling. As I drove to the Whitneys' home, I shivered, despite my heavy wool coat, thick scarf and leather gloves.

When I arrived a few minutes before the scheduled showing, Donna ushered me into the foyer. "You must be freezing!" she said as she hung up my coat and led me toward the fireplace.

"It's cold out there. The high today is only supposed to be in the twenties," I concurred.

"Mary, would you like for me to leave while you show the house?" Donna asked.

"Heavens, no! Not in this weather."

"I'll stay out of your way. If you need me, I'll be in the library," she said and disappeared as the door bell rang. I opened the door and ushered in a middle-aged couple.

"Hello," I said warmly. "Please come in and get out of the cold! I'm Mary. You must be May and Bob Knoll. May I take your wraps?"

"If you don't mind, we'll keep them on."

"Shall we start in the living room, which features a warm fireplace. I think we could all use a little warmth."

They laughed as we headed toward the fireplace. I quickly pointed out the cut stone mantel and beautiful walnut woodwork. The Knolls tarried by the warm fire as I called their attention to the beveled windows and the wide window sills. The dining room spoke for itself, with the built-in china cupboard and paneled wainscoting.

Entering the library, I introduced the Knolls to Mrs. Whitney but otherwise I continued to point out the quality of craftsmanship, already a lost art. I also commented that a home of this quality could not be reproduced for twice the asking price. I noticed that Donna's ears perked up as I described her home. She followed me to the basement to help get the lights on and remained while I pointed out the benefits of their hot water heating system – one that I wanted in my own home, but couldn't afford, so much healthier than gas.

When I finished showing the home, Mr. and Mrs. Knoll thanked me, commenting that they liked the home and would think about it and get back to me if they became more interested.

The next morning, as I was cleaning up the kitchen after breakfast, the phone rang. "I'll get it," I announced, then sprang to the phone.

It was Bob Knoll. He disclosed that they were definitely interested in the Whitney home and would like to meet with me about making an offer. They wanted to offer three hundred and sixty thousand dollars. After discussing the offer with Mr. Fuller, he assured me that it was a fair offer to present to the Whitneys.

That evening, as I stood shivering on the Whitneys' porch waiting for them to answer the doorbell, my gloved hand clutched the signed contract and my heart beat rapidly. I couldn't wait to see the Whitneys' excitement at selling their home so quickly.

"Hello, Mary," Donna greeted me.

"You won't believe it, Mrs. Whitney, I already have a contract for the purchase of your home." Mr. and Mrs. Whitney smiled politely, but neither of them showed any sign of excitement. "The couple I took through the house last night have made an offer."

"Would you like to sit down, Mary?" Mr. Whitney asked, as he led me into the living room. I sat down, frowning and confused. "You've done a wonderful job of selling our house, and we appreciate your work, but we have been doing a lot of thinking today and we have decided not to sell our home."

"WHAT?" My eyes widened and eyebrows raised.

"Well," Mrs. Whitney took over, "to tell the truth, when I heard you touring the house with the Knolls yesterday, I realized that we were crazy to think of leaving this home. You were absolutely right when you said that you could never build a home like this today for the price and that the craftsmanship could never be duplicated. This house is very unique and I suppose we didn't appreciate it until we heard you emphasize all of its beautiful features."

THAT EXPERIENCE TAUGHT ME A LESSON I WILL NEVER FORGET. "NEVER HAVE THE OWNERS PRESENT WHEN YOU SHOW THEIR HOME, REGARDLESS OF THE WEATHER."

DISAPPOINTMENT

In the three years since I started selling real estate I had made some good commissions, which I had immediately invested in furniture for our home. When I received my most recent commission check, I promised myself I would put it in the bank for my dream trip to Oberammergau. But instead, I purchased a couch for the living room that I had been eyeing for a long time. Besides, I consoled myself, I had four more years to earn the money for the trip. The next performance would be not until 1960.

It was summertime, which meant a lot of activity for the children. My agreement with Mr. Fuller was that I could name my own hours, so it was easy to convince him to take me off of board duty for the summer. Now I could enjoy both worlds – more time with my family and friends, and real estate when it was convenient.

One day at the pool, while the children were taking their swimming lessons, I sat basking in the sun visiting with several other mothers.

Susie, one of the women, asked me how real estate was going. I informed her that I was taking some time off to enjoy my family. She continued, "The reason I asked is that my husband just hired a new office manager and I thought you might like to show them Kansas City and what was available in real estate." My adrenaline surged. "I'd be delighted and would love the opportunity." Susie said she would check with Bud, her husband, and have him call if he hadn't made other arrangements.

The next morning before breakfast was over, Bud called. The people were arriving the following weekend and planned to stay for a week to look for a home. With some directions from Bud as to their price bracket, I knew I could find them a home.

Mr. and Mrs. Elliott were coming in from New York City. When I picked them up at the airport, the first thing Mrs. Elliott asked, in her distinctive New York accent, was, "Do you have any place where I can get my French poodle groomed?" This was the first time they had ever been west of the Hudson River, so they were a bit skeptical about the area. I quickly retorted, "Sure, we even sell them here." We both laughed. I already knew it was going to be fun working with the Elliotts.

I had arranged for them to see a home that I had not previewed. To my surprise, two standard French poodles greeted us at the front door. That immediately convinced Mrs. Elliott that Kansas City was "uptown."

After showing them several homes, they both decided on one in Leawood. It was charming and impeccably furnished. The window treatments in the living and dining rooms were exceptionally elegant, made of a very expensive brocade.

I prepared the contract, which was very close to the asking price, and it was immediately accepted by the sellers. The closing date was three months away, which gave the sellers time to arrange their out-of-town move.

In the meantime the Elliotts went back to New York City and I took care of the inspections and getting the utilities transferred to their name, which pleased Mr. Elliott, who was going to be busy with his new job.

Soon all the necessary inspections were in order. The Elliotts were unable to be in town for the closing, so my office handled everything through the mail. The seller closed at our office, at which time they left the keys and garage door openers with the closing secretary.

But this otherwise easy and pleasant sale ended up becoming my first disappointment in a real-estate transaction and in people. I had promised the Elliotts that I would arrange to have the lawn mowed before they moved to Kansas City, which would be a month after closing. When I met the lawn man to check his work and pay him, I decided to check out the home at the same time. To my disappointment and surprise, the beautiful brocaded curtains were gone, replaced by new cheap ones. I was furious and immediately called the sellers. I talked with the wife, who promised her husband would call me back.

Several days later I received a letter from the sellers stating that the contract only specified that all window curtains remain. They had left the curtains that were in the home when they purchased it. How dishonest!

I could not tell the Elliotts that those beautiful draperies were not there, so I spent my commission replacing them.

I LEARNED A BIG LESSON. ANY CONTRACT STATING THAT ALL WINDOW TREATMENTS ARE INCLUDED MUST READ, "ALL DRAPERIES NOW IN THE HOME ARE INCLUDED."

BUYERS MAY BE LIARS

One thing I learned early in the business was to listen to what my clients wanted and not show them homes that didn't match their requisites.

One time I was working with a couple from Chicago. The wife, an interior decorator, was very precise about what she was looking for in a home. The one thing she insisted on was large bedrooms. This was a must!

As a result, I was very careful to check the sizes of the bedrooms before showing them any homes. After working with this client for several days, I was still unable to show her anything that excited her. There was one home I knew she would like, but it had exceptionally small bedrooms. The master bedroom was twelve by fifteen feet and the other bedrooms were so small they barely held a double bed and a chest. However, it had charm and lots of innovative features. I had shown the home several times before and always loved it, but wondered why the owners had designed it with such small bedrooms.

I decided to drive the client past the home after all, and before I could tell her that the bedrooms were too small, she said she wanted to see it. I decided not to say a word about the size of the bedrooms. The home was unoccupied so we could see it immediately.

The living room was very dramatic, with a high vaulted ceiling, enhanced by a large stone fireplace. For the first time the client showed some excitement. She became even more excited when she entered the dining room, which featured a cozy fireplace and a natural slate floor. As I ushered the clients into the kitchen, the wife turned to her husband and announced that she wanted to buy the home.

"But, you haven't seen the bedrooms yet," I interrupted. "They are very small and that is why I never showed you this home before." As they walked into the master bedroom, the wife looked around quietly as I stepped back to capture her reaction. "Well, it is small, but let's face it, you only sleep in the bedroom."

I promptly sold them the home and they were very happy.

Another client, who was moving to Kansas City from Philadelphia, was referred to me by a friend. When I met Mr. Carlton, I was surprised to learn that he was interested in buying a farm. He explained, "I was raised on a farm and I have always wanted to buy one and now is a good time since my job will keep me here in the midwest."

His wife, who was expecting their third child, would not be joining him for a month. This would give me the time I needed to look for farms. It was a challenge, as I knew nothing about farms.

Since Charles was raised on a farm, I thought it would be a great idea to have a dinner party and invite Tom Carlton. It turned out to be a great evening.

I promised Tom I would research some farms and get back to him to set up a time to show him. Tom in turn assured me he would not look at any farms without me. I did my homework. I checked the newspapers and, with the help of farm agents and Charles, decided which ones would be good buys.

It was springtime and the farms were beautiful. One weekend, I asked Charles to join Tom and me as we toured the area, and Charles was more than happy to comply. He and Tom had a great day checking out two farms. Even I thought it would be great to live on a farm – being a city girl, I didn't realize how much work owning a farm could be.

Several weeks later, Tom called to tell me that his wife would be in Kansas City the following weekend. By this time, Tom was like a member of the family. We made breakfast plans so I could meet Carol, who was just as pleasant as her husband.

The waiter had just poured our first cup of coffee when Carol turned to me and said, "Mary, Tom has been telling me about the farms you have been showing him. I know he wants a farm, but seriously this is not the time to buy a farm. I'm seven months pregnant, with two little ones besides. I need to be close to a hospital, schools and shopping. I promised Tom that when the children are grown, we will definitely buy a farm."

The next couple of days I showed Carol homes and ended up selling them one in Johnson county within walking distance of schools. After all the time we spent looking at farms, without them buying one, Tom and Carol became very good friends with Charles and me.

Besides, the time we spent looking for farms with Tom and Carol didn't totally go to waste. Charles kept looking at farm ads and one day when he came home from work he said he wanted to show me something. "I'm not going to tell you what it is, so stop asking. It's a surprise," he teased. The following Saturday, Charles drove me to the country to show me a farm. We didn't buy it, but he kept looking. Finally we found the right place and became the owners of a farm and raised white-faced Herefords. We hired a manager for the farm and became weekend farmers.

Farms are wonderful – quiet – but a lot of work. Besides, with the midwest weather so unpredictable, I constantly found myself praying either for rain, or for the rain to stop so our ponds wouldn't overflow!

BUYERS MAY BE LIARS, BUT SOMETIMES THEY CAN SHOW YOU A WHOLE NEW WAY OF LIFE.

PRAYER AND FAITH

The children had been hustled out the door as the bus turned our corner – well bundled up in hats, gloves and boots. The temperature was predicted to drop to the low teens by the afternoon. Already the snow flakes were falling heavily.

I was alone now, staring out of the kitchen window at a world that was quickly turning white. The snow was becoming heavier and prettier by the minute. I loved the snow. It made the world so peaceful and serene.

I gradually floated back to the kitchen sink and the breakfast dishes and remembered why I had gotten into real estate four years earlier. This decision was primarily to earn enough commissions to finance my dream trip to Oberammergau. All of my plans for the trip were now made. Charles couldn't take the time from his office to join me, plus he wasn't that interested in seeing the play. But he fully supported my going. He and Grandmother Overfelt would care for the children while I was gone. I had persuaded one of my girlfriends to join me and we were both looking forward to a fun time together.

Early on, the sales came fast and the commissions were good. It seemed so easy and soon the monies needed for the trip were earned. But then came the expensive couch. Just a few more sales would replenish the funds required for the trip, I told myself. Soon afterwards I decided the children must have a set of encyclopedias. And over the years, with the children's needs and decorating the home, the bank account marked "Oberammergau" had gradually dwindled.

The calendar indicated it was January 1960. Plans had been in place for over a year – tickets were purchased and our passports ready. The trip was less than five months away. I only needed one more sale to have enough funds to go.

"Will the winter be so bad this year that no one will venture out to buy a home," I thought. Past winters had turned out to be good for my business. But this year I had no immediate prospects. The snow was falling heavily, with all indications that it was to be a lasting blizzard. I looked out the window at the cloudy heavens and said a prayer. "Dear God, please help me make one more sale." I waited a second and added, "Dear God, if it's thy will." I remembered that my father always added those words to his prayers. Then I whispered to myself, "Please make it thy will, dear Lord."

Before I got started with the rest of my morning chores, the telephone rang. It was Mr. Guy Pine, our neighbor. In a surprised tone, I asked, "What's going on, Guy?"

"Mary, I'm interested in the piece of property on the corner of 103rd and State Line. Will you check it out for me and see what they are asking for it. I want to buy it if the price is right."

"Sure. I'll check it out immediately and call you back." I knew the property he was referring to. I bundled up and headed out right away. As I drove out of the driveway, I looked to heaven and thanked God. I had faith that God would answer my prayer, but I was surprised he answered it so quickly.

As I pulled into the driveway of the property Guy had mentioned, I saw it had a Paul Hamilton real-estate sign in the yard. I was hoping it wasn't an exclusive listing. I traipsed through the snow and after ringing the doorbell was greeted by a pleasant, elderly gentleman. "I'm sorry to bother you.

I'm Mary Overfelt, and I am in the real-estate business. I have a client who is interested in purchasing your property. Is it listed exclusively with Paul Hamilton's company?"

"Indeed, it is not! The exclusive is up, and besides, they haven't shown it for weeks. I told them to get the sign out of the yard. I'm Jack Maloney, won't you come in out of the cold?"

My adrenalin started flowing. I reviewed the property, most important of which was the price. The property consisted of a large home, a barn and ten acres. Jack was excited about my prospect and about having a visitor, so he cheerfully showed me the house. His wife had died the year before and he wasn't able to keep the property up since his arthritis was getting worse. When we got to the den, he proudly showed me his old player piano. I had heard of them but had never seen one.

"Would you like me to play for you?" he asked hopefully. "I would love it," I replied genuinely. For the next hour I sat on the piano bench next to Jack, listening attentively as he pumped away on the pedals.

I finally got Jack to sign an exclusive with me. Thanking him, I promised I would get back to him shortly. On the way out I made sure to remove the Paul Hamilton sign and promptly put up my own.

I called Guy immediately. Not knowing my urgency for a sale, he was pleased that I had taken care of his assignment so quickly during a snow storm. He was not interested in the condition of the home or the barn. He was only interested in the land and its location for future development.

In about two weeks, Mr. Pine owned the property and I had more than sufficient funds for my Oberammergau trip. But I still had a problem. The sale was not to close until June 10, and I was scheduled to leave May 10.

I decided to make an appointment with my banker. I showed him my contract. Knowing Mr. Pine, and the piece of property, he was quick to lend me the amount of my commission in advance. I could now relax – I was all set for my trip.

I celebrated my fortieth birthday, May 18, with my friend in a very quaint old pub in Oberammergau. The next day, we saw the season's first performance of the famous passion play. As I sat in the open theater looking up with the Alps in the distance, I started to cry with joy. I had finally made it. Closing my eyes, I thanked God again.

I LEARNED THAT WITH A LOT OF DETERMINATION I HAD BEEN ABLE TO REACH MY GOAL – TO ATTEND THE OBERAMMERGAU PASSION PLAY.

EXPANDING

Heading home after my wonderful trip to the Oberammergau passion play and several other exciting spots in Europe, I was reminded that the only reason I had gotten into real estate five years earlier was so that I could make enough money to go to the passion play. Now, that my dream had come true, would I continue in the real-estate business? I enjoyed it, but it took a lot of time away from my family and friends.

I loved to sell, and I was good at it. In reviewing my sales I discovered that, except for one or two sales, I had originated the clients and had found the home that pleased them without any help from my office. I was very confident in my ability to sell – I was honest and that was reflected immediately in my personality. Also, I was a hard worker and had a lot of determination.

This was nothing new. As a child of around ten, I sold salt water taffy from door to door on Saturdays. I tried hard to establish regular customers by giving them a free bag after they had bought a certain number of bags.

It was difficult to get up early in the morning for school during the week, but never on Saturday. I was up early to pick up my candy at the wholesale factory and usually had everything sold by noon.

One Saturday afternoon when I was counting my profits, my brother, who was three years younger than me, looked on enviously. "Mary, could I help you some time?" "Sure, come along next Saturday," I promised.

The following Saturday, I gave Paul the opposite side of the street to work. Not long after we had started, Paul came across the street to me with tears in his eyes. "A lady slammed the door in my face." I gave him no sympathy but merely said, "Go on to the next house." That was the last time Paul begged me to let him help. I looked back on those days as being wonderful.

Thinking back, an idea was born. Why not get my broker's license and open my own office? I could have the best of both worlds that way – call my own hours and make all the commission.

After the excitement of arriving home, sharing my trip with my family and giving the gifts I had bought for them – a small HO train from Germany for Rocky and dolls from the various countries for Leslie – I took time to review my thoughts about starting my own company.

After dinner one night, I approached Charles about my idea. "I thought you liked Mr. Fuller?" was his response. "I do, but just think, most of my leads I have gotten myself. I have found the homes myself and he has gotten fifty percent of the commission. I hate board duty and I dislike the attitude of so many of my co-workers. They care more about their commission than about finding the right home for their clients. I actually heard one girl brag that she didn't tell her client until the contract was signed that the home he was buying was situated on a septic tank. The other day Mr. Fuller called me aside and warned me not to mention any clients I was working with, insinuating that one of my co-workers might try to steal them. I told him if my co-workers could steal my clients, then I wasn't doing a good job. Mr. Fuller just smiled."

"Mary, don't misunderstand me," Charles responded. " I think it's a great idea. As for the office space, I have room for another desk in my office." I leaned over and kissed Charles who was as supportive as ever.

The next challenge was to tell Mr. Fuller about my decision. I dreaded the thought. I called the office and set up an appointment with him. Mr. Fuller agreed to see me whenever it suited me. Since I wanted to get it over with as soon as possible, I made plans to see him that afternoon.

When I entered his office, he was in a very friendly mood, probably expecting I was there to tell of another great listing or a sale I needed his help with. When I announced that I was going to get my broker's license and wanted to work independently, his friendly mood soon changed to an appalling, offensive one. He was shocked that I thought I was ready for that jump and tried to discourage me. "Mary, there is more to real estate than selling. For example, you need connections for financing." Unstoppable, I replied, "Mr. Fuller, if I have a client with money in his pocket, I'm sure any bank will be willing to take it."

"I guess you're right, Mary," he replied. "But you're going to need a closer."

I reminded him that I had a good attorney and I had already talked to a title company that would close my transactions. With those answers, Mr. Fuller gave me his blessing. I thanked him for all his help and told him I had enjoyed working for his company.

I then proceeded to clean out my desk, thankful that Melva wasn't in the office that afternoon to ask a million questions. But news travels fast. I had not been home more than an hour when Melva called to ask her usual nosy questions. I explained my reasoning for leaving the Fuller Company, which satisfied her. Then, in a very clandestine tone, she said she would like to work for me. I was set back for a second before I replied. "Thanks, Melva, for wanting to work for me, but at present I am not ready to hire agents, and maybe I never will."

Opening my own office seemed to be the next natural step in my career as a real-estate agent.

LISTENING TO MY "GUT" INSTINCTS HAS ALWAYS PAID OFF.

INDISCREET

The summer was over and the children were back in school. Now I had to think about getting my office in order and looking for business. Even though I had sworn I was retreating for the summer, I was a little disappointed that no one had called during the summer months.

As I stepped into the shower one morning, the telephone rang. My first impulse was to ignore it, but I quickly wrapped myself in a towel and stepped into the bedroom to answer the phone.

Telephones haunted me. In my business they were important tools. Especially now that I was my own broker, I didn't dare ignore a phone call.

"Hello," I answered in a soft business voice, not letting on that I was caught off guard. It turned out to be Dale, my brother-in-law, who owned the Uptown Interlude, a popular restaurant and night club in midtown Kansas City. Jokingly I said, "Do you want to buy a home, Dale?"

He laughed, "No! But I have a customer for you. He is staying across the street at the Ambassador Hotel and eats here every night. I was visiting with him last night when he mentioned that he was moving to Kansas City and had to start looking for a home. I told him about you and gave him your number. His name is Mike Dickens. He said he would call you."

"Thanks, Dale! I'm ready for a customer."

Sure enough, Mike called later that morning. After introducing himself, he mentioned that Dale had said I would be the best person to help him find a home.

"I'll do my best. First, tell me exactly what you are looking for in a home. How many are in your family, what size of investment do you want to make, and what else is important to you and your family?"

As Mike spoke, I took careful notes and I soon had a good understanding of what he was looking for. Namely, he wanted a two-story colonial home near good schools for his four children ranging in age from six to eleven.

"Give me a couple of days to line up some homes for you to review before your wife gets to town," I ended our conversation.

I spent the next two days searching the market for the perfect home for Mr. and Mrs. Dickens. Sure enough, I found one I became quite excited about as it fit all the requisites Mike had mentioned. It was a brick, two-story with green shutters and white trim. It had a low picket fence covered with Floribunda roses, which were trying desperately to bloom in the cool spring weather. The home was in Prairie Village, known for its good schools and filled with other young families.

I called Mike immediately, and his secretary put me through right away. "Mike Dickens," he answered in a very professional tone. "Hello, Mr. Dickens," I said, unable to hide the excitement in my voice. "I've found a few homes for you to look at, and among them, there's one I think you will find just perfect."

"Wonderful!"

"When would you be available to look at them?"

"Mary, would it be possible for you to meet me at the Interlude, as I am very busy here at the plant during the day." I agreed to meet him at five o'clock that evening.

I gave Mike a review of the homes I wanted to show him, and took pictures of the one in Prairie Village. He agreed that would be the one his wife would like the most.

"You have done a great job, Mary. My wife will be in town next weekend. Unfortunately, I'll be buried at the office and will not have time to look at the homes before she arrives."

"Well, then, why don't we all plan to see them together when she arrives?"

"Great. How about picking up Glenda and me at nine o'clock at the hotel next Saturday?"

"Fine. I'll see you then."

"Oh, and Mary ... don't say anything to Glenda about my being too busy to look at the houses. She just doesn't understand how busy I am at work and it would probably start an unnecessary argument. She thinks I spend too much time at the office as it is."

"Fair enough. We'll keep it a secret."

The next Saturday I met them in the lobby of the Ambassador Hotel promptly at nine. Glenda was a delightful person. "It's so nice to meet you, Mary," she said, as soon as her husband had introduced us. "Mike said he has found the perfect home for us but won't tell me anything about it. He said it's a surprise. I can't wait to see it. You know, Mary, I don't think I'll miss Cincinnati much. We've only lived there for a few years anyway and I've never felt attached to it. But, I will miss our home. It's beautiful! It's a white colonial two-story. It will be hard to leave it, but I know I'll like the homes you and Mike have found here. I can't wait to see the one Mike feels is perfect for us."

"Well, I hope you like it," I said, as I led them to my car. I took them through four homes that met most of their criteria, each one of which Glenda seemed to like. I saved for last the one I thought fit their needs and was in the best location. When we pulled into the driveway of that home, Glenda gasped with delight.

"Oh, my goodness, Mike," she whispered, as she gazed up at the two-story home. "And it's all brick – this is it!"

"Well, this is the one Mike said you would like the best," I said as we got out of the car. I stole a glance at Mike just in time to see him wink surreptitiously.

As we toured the home, Glenda gasped, ooh'd and sighed with pleasure. "It's perfect," she said, as we stood in the foyer after touring the home. "I can't believe it. I would even go as far as to say that this is better than our home in Cincinnati."

"I knew you would like it, honey, the minute I laid eyes on it," Mike responded.

Mike gave me another quick wink and then put his arm around his wife's shoulders. Glenda kissed him and said, "You've done a perfect job."

After Mike and Glenda had closed on their new home, I called my brother-in-law to thank him for sending them to me.

"Tell me, Mary, what was his wife like?" he asked.

"A very charming woman.Why did you ask?"

"He's been having an affair with Sandy every since he came to town."

"You mean Sandy, the piano player?"

"Yeah. That's how I've gotten to know him. He's in here every night."

I rolled my eyes and slapped my palm against my forehead. "That's why he didn't have time to look at homes," I mumbled under my breath.

When I got into real estate I had no idea of the types of situations I would find myself in.

I SOON LEARNED ANOTHER VALUABLE LESSON:
TO BE VERY DISCREET!

MAKING MY OWN RULES

I enjoyed having my own company – I could make my own rules, and I did. For example, I decided never to take a listing from somebody unless I had sold them a home and later they were transferred. People who were selling homes were usually not realistic about their price. So often an agent would work a listing very hard and still not be able to get the price lowered, and then invariably the owner would give it to another agent, lower the price – and the home would sell.

I also decided not to spend much time with local buyers as they took too long to make a decision. It never takes me long to decide on things. Therefore, it was very hard for me to understand people looking for a home for two or more years. Such people were lookers, and there were a lot of lookers out there. If they found the home that had everything they were looking for, in the perfect neighborhood, and the price was right, they just might buy.

It was hard for me to work with indecisive people. I always know what I want, so decisions are easy for me. In fact, I bought one of our own homes at a cocktail party. The person who owned it had shown it to me when he was decorating it to seek my opinion. I loved it and told him that, if he ever decided to sell, to please let me know. Years later Charles and I were invited to a cocktail party at the same home. During the evening Kip, the owner, called me aside and said he was going to sell. "Are you interested?" he asked. "Sure, but let me check with Charles."

I got Charles on the side and informed him that Kip was going to sell and asked if we could buy the home. Charles, who by then had had several martinis, knew that I knew what I was doing when it came to real estate, so he said "sure." I promptly relayed the answer to Kip.

The next morning Charles jumped out of bed to ask one question: "Honey, what kind of a furnace does that home have?" "Oh! Charles," I laughed, "when you pay that kind of money for a home, if you don't like the furnace you simply buy a new one. Seriously, don't worry, honey, we'll have everything checked. Besides, Kip keeps his home in excellent condition." After breakfast that same morning we met Kip and wrote a contract. I knew what I wanted and bought it!

A lead I got one day from a Ford dealership where Charles bought all his cars made me decide how I would sell real estate. A new district manager, Mr. English, was coming to town. I called Detroit immediately and introduced myself to Mr. English. Evidently, my telephone voice was convincing as Mr. English made plans for me to pick him up at the airport. I worked very hard to find the home that would please Mr. and Mrs. English. The day they moved in, I sent my housekeeper over to help Mrs. English and also had the *Kansas City Star* delivered for Mr. English. Needless to say, I impressed Mr. English and from then on sold a home to every Ford employee who was transferred to Kansas City.

Through the Ford Company I subsequently got American Motor Company's (AMC) business – since several Ford executives were enticed to join AMC.

One time as I was leaving home for the airport to pick up the new district manager for AMC, I decided it would be impressive to pick him up in an American Motors car. I pulled into the AMC dealership on Wornall Road. I told the manager whom I was picking up and asked if I could borrow one of his cars, at the same time handing him the keys to my Lincoln. No questions were asked and I soon drove off in their latest model. What an easy way to do business in those days. Today this would never have happened.

As the new district manager jumped into the new AMC model at the airport, he smiled and asked me how I liked my car. "I love it," I quickly responded. About a mile from the airport it started to rain, which had not been in the weather forecast. I panicked, as I desperately searched for the windshield wipers. Where were they in this model? The traffic was heavy, making it hard to both concentrate on the other cars and find the wipers.

"Where are the wipers in this car?" I finally asked. The client reached over on the dash and solved the problem immediately. In a questioning tone he burst out, "Don't you know where the wipers are?" "Actually, no," I calmly replied. "I just picked this car up at an AMC dealership to impress you and I didn't have time to check anything out. I didn't want to pick you up in my Lincoln," I said apologetically. The client smiled and thanked me for my thoughtfulness.

I sold him a home and took care of all AMC's transfers from then on. By the way, the AMC man was a good salesman too. Before he was transferred, he sold me a Jeep for our farm.

MY COMPANY GREW AND PROSPERED BECAUSE I NOT ONLY MADE MY OWN RULES – I FOLLOWED THEM.

PERSISTENCE

Stubbornness is not in my personality unless some one challenges me. I was challenged one day by a lawyer. I had sold a home that was on a small lake in Leawood. In closing the transaction the title work revealed that in order to sell any property on that lake I had to get all the owners (five) on the lake to sign a certain document regarding conditions of the lake. The lawyer who was representing my buyers called to inform me that it would be impossible to close on the date of the contract since one of the owners on the lake was on a cruise in the Mediterranean and wouldn't be back for weeks. The closing date was paramount to my clients since they would be arriving in Kansas City with four little children and one on the way.

In my efforts to reach the owner, one of the neighbors gave me the name of the cruise line. I called the captain on the ship and after explaining my situation, asked him if I cabled a certain important paper to be signed by one of his passengers he would notarize it for me. He agreed. Then I asked to talk to that passenger. After explaining the situation to him, who thank goodness was very agreeable to signing the release, I received the papers back the next morning only to prove to the lawyer that we could close on the stated date.

Several days after we closed the transaction the lawyer wrote a very kind letter thanking me for my diligence and ending the letter by saying, "If you want anything done, give it to Mary Overfelt."

Two years after I had gotten the legal matter corrected concerning the lake, the owners were transferred to another state and asked me to sell the home for a second time.

At the time Leawood was one of the most popular suburban areas of Kansas City. It was developed by Kroh Brothers, a large development company with their own real-estate agency. So, if you wanted to buy a home there, you had to go to their agency. However, if an owner wanted to resell his home, he could pick any company to sell it. In those days Kroh Brothers only hired men in their real-estate office, and they never co-opped with other real-estate agents.

A gentleman answered my ad on the home and made an appointment to review it. After he spent some time checking everything, he said he thought the home would be perfect for him and his family. They had just adopted three little children ages three, four and six. The home would suit their needs and he wanted to buy it.

"Don't you want your wife to see it?" I said. "Oh, she will like it. And besides she is too busy learning how to care for these children," he replied matter-of-factly. I then suggested that maybe she might object to the lake with three little ones. But there was no turning back. "Oh no! I'm going to teach them how to swim," came the reply.

Shortly after I made the sale, I ran into one of Kroh Brothers salesmen, a friend of mine. He said, "Mary, we got hell because of you at our sales meeting yesterday."

"Why me?" I asked.

"Because you sold that Johnson home twice." He laughed and told me one of the salesmen got up and said, "She sells them because she wines them and dines them. Our sales manager ended our meeting by saying, 'Go wine them and dine them.'"

I MAY WINE AND DINE CLIENTS, BUT I'M MOST PROUD OF HOW I LISTEN TO THEIR NEEDS AND FIND THEM A PLACE TO CALL HOME.

THE PEONY BUSH

I once had a client who wanted a very contemporary home. At the time this was not an easy thing to find in Kansas City, which had few contemporary homes. But after some searching, I finally found one in my client's price bracket. When I previewed the home, I discovered that it had a very commodious floor plan but was not kept in good condition.

I showed the home to my clients who liked the floor plan and wanted to buy the house in spite of the dirty condition. It was so bad that there was even dog do-do in the corner of one bedroom when I showed it. All I could say was, "It's obvious they have a dog." Their calm response was, "True. We'll just have the place exterminated before we move in."

When we wrote a contract, we deducted enough from the asking price to cover the cleanup. The offer was accepted by the sellers except for one condition. The owner was very emphatic that a peony bush in the backyard given to her by her mother was not to go with the sale. That was no problem, as my client could care less. We were closing in the spring, which was a bad time to move the bush, so an addendum was drawn up by the owners' lawyer stating that the peony bush would remain in the backyard until October 1, at which time it would be removed by the owners. My clients' lawyer reviewed the addendum and added that if the bush was not removed by that date, it could not be removed later. After making many trips back and forth to the sellers' and buyers' lawyers, I finally got a contract signed by all parties.

Soon thereafter the buyers moved in, redid the home and were very happy. When fall came, they never heard a word from the sellers concerning the peony bush, which is still in the backyard today.

DESPITE WHAT EVERYBODY SAYS, SOMETIMES YOU HAVE TO SWEAT THE SMALL THINGS!

THOUGHTFULNESS

I had no desire to be the top real-estate lady in Kansas City, but I wanted to be the best! My pride would never let me lose a client. I worked hard not only to find the home that suited my clients but also followed through to help out until they moved in. For example, for those clients coming from out of town, I would make sure the utilities were transferred to their names ahead of time. It soon became clear that it was all the service I extended "beyond the call of duty" that landed me all my referrals.

When families moved with small children, I often took care of the children the day they moved in to relieve the mother. I would take the children out to lunch, and if the weather permitted I sometimes took them to the zoo. The children – and the parents – loved me.

One day I was shopping in the Plaza and a very young, handsome man stopped me on the street. "Pardon me, you are Mary Overfelt, aren't you?" I smiled and nodded. "I'm Billy Bartlett. You sold my mother and father a home many years ago. I was only seven then, but I recognized you and your hat. I still remember the day when we pulled up to our new home in Kansas City. You were there waiting for us with a big pot of coffee. With mother's most grateful permission, you ushered my sister and me off for a fun day that I never forgot. First you took us to the zoo and then out for lunch. You took us to a hamburger place on State Line." After recovering from my surprise, I responded, "Billy, you sure grew up to be a handsome man. Tell me about your sister and parents."

After visiting for a few minutes, we decided to stop at a nearby coffee shop where we enjoyed a long reminiscing chat.

I gave more than just service – it was a deep caring and thoughtfulness that people remembered me for.

The Thomas family from Seattle, Washington, were another referral that stands out in my mind. They made it clear that they wanted a home with lots of trees. I showed them many houses they liked but they were always disappointed with the lack of trees. Finally, they decided to forget trees and focus on the home. The home they decided on had a beautiful, landscaped yard but no trees. When they returned to Kansas City with their furniture, I surprised them by planting a huge tree in their front yard. It was the largest tree I could find that could be replanted.

The morning they moved into their new home, Mr. Thomas said to the movers. "Wait, this is the wrong home. Ours didn't have a tree in the front yard." I drove up just in time to say, "It does now! Welcome to Kansas City." The Thomases enjoyed the home for many years before they were transferred back to Seattle.

Many years later I received a letter from a real-estate agent in Seattle named Nancy Thomas. Nancy mentioned in her letter that she had gotten into real estate because of me. She referred to their pleasant move to Kansas City and how her mother and father were so pleased with the tree I had planted for them. "This gave me the idea of planting a tree for every client I sell a home to, although not quite as big as the one you planted for mother and daddy. They never stopped talking about that tree. Thanks, Mary, for setting a good example of thoughtfulness," she ended her note.

THOUGHTFULNESS ALWAYS PAYS OFF.

VISITING THE PRINCE OF JORDAN

In the early seventies I had an opportunity to list for sale a large horse farm owned by a family who trained and showed horses all over the world. The original owner had died, and since he and his wife had no children, the estate had been passed on to their nephews. Rich in their own right, the heirs had little interest in the horse farm, which consequently had fallen into neglect. Upon the advice of the lawyer for the estate, I got the listing to sell the property.

When I was reading the newspaper one morning, an article caught my attention. An ex-army officer was bringing a hundred horses owned by the prince of Jordan to Kansas City. He had promised the prince that he would start horse racing in Kansas City. I immediately called the gentleman, hoping I could sell him the farm for the prince's horses. The gentleman was enthusiastic about the idea and wanted to meet with me.

When we met, he was quick to show me a note for $700,000 from the prince of Jordan, thus establishing his ability to buy the farm. During our conversation he mentioned that he was also looking for a home for the prince since he would be coming to Kansas City often and would want a residence. I showed him several homes from which he picked one in Sunset Hills, just south of the Plaza. The price was $250,000. He thought it would be perfect for the prince but suggested that we sell it to him for $500,000. "The prince wouldn't know the difference," he reasoned.

I immediately told him I would be no part of such a transaction. "The price is $250,000 and that is it," I concluded and proceeded to write the contract for that amount. He signed it and gave me a thousand dollar deposit.

All I could think about that evening was how dishonest this man was whom the prince had placed his trust in. I couldn't get him out of my mind and decided to call Washington and talk to the ambassador from Jordan. When I revealed the truth about this man, the ambassador asked me to write a letter explaining everything. Within a week a representative from Jordan came to Kansas City to visit me.

The prince was not moving to Kansas City. Apparently, he had met this impostor at the race tracks in London. Since the man introduced himself as a retired U.S. army officer, the prince had trusted him. After tearing up the contract and the check, I invited the royal representative to dinner at the Kansas City Club with my family. He was most thankful for the evening and that I had so graciously torn up the signed contract and check.

But the story didn't end there. After hearing of my actions, the prince invited me to Amman as his guest! Naturally, I was thrilled and immediately accepted the invitation. Unfortunately, Charles could not take the time from his work to join me. I couldn't miss this opportunity and since I didn't want to go alone, I enticed a girlfriend to join me.

In Amman, the prince had an escort awaiting our arrival. During the eleven days we spent in Jordan we had a Mercedes, a driver and a gracious Jordanian lady to escort us. The entire visit was spectacular.

When the prince asked me what I wanted to do first, I replied that I would like to visit the countryside and see how the Bedouins live. The prince was a fabulous host. He planned a day in the countryside, including a Bedouin-style picnic. I was fascinated by the unique way they eat their food. First, they wash their hands thoroughly, then they pick up the food with their hands and shoot it into their mouths. Supposedly, this is more sanitary than our way of putting the spoon into our mouths and back into the food. Never shy or afraid to try something new, I ate like the Bedouins.

Also new to me was the custom that if you admire something in Jordan, they give it to you. Consequently, I have a beautiful antique chest in my living room, which arrived by airmail in Kansas City upon my return.

The whole trip was a fairy tale, including the last evening when clear out of the blue the prince asked me to be his third wife! Before I could get my wits together to respond, he went on, "I know you wouldn't want to live in Amman, but you could live in Paris or London." He realized I was in shock – and believe me, I was! After composing myself a little, I took his hand and told him I was flattered, but that my religion allowed only one husband. I already had one, Charles, whom I loved and I couldn't love two men at one time. Later that night we all, including his second wife, went out to dinner together.

THIS EXTRAORDINARY EXPERIENCE PROMPTED ME TO CONSIDER THE FOLLOWING REWRITE OF THE OLD SAYING: "THERE ARE TIMES, WHEN LOOKING A GIFT HORSE IN THE MOUTH IS INDEED THE BETTER STRATEGY."

CHARTWELL – THE BEGINNING OF A NEW ERA

During the 1970s Charles and I enjoyed our country French two-story home off Ward Parkway in the Country Club area. However, recently there had been several robberies in our neighborhood. Even though our home was secured by an alarm system, the thought of prowlers was disturbing.

While lying awake one night, I got the idea of building a small group of residential homes, surrounding them with a wall and securing the area with gates. When I told Charles he agreed it was a great idea, never thinking that I was going to run with it.

My first step was to find a tract of land. That could prove to be a problem. It would have to be within the city limits and close to shopping. I immediately started my search. After driving around for hours, I realized that a small tract of vacant land did not exist in any desirous area. However, I did notice the corner at 95th and State Line with two dilapidated vacant homes on it. I drove into the driveway of one of them, and to my delight discovered that the lots were much larger than they had appeared from the street.

As I was walking the lots, one of the neighbors appeared to check on what I was doing. "I was wondering who owned these two homes," I explained. "The McGilley Funeral Homes," he shouted back at me. "They bought the land to build another funeral home but they couldn't get it zoned. We neighbors got together and really gave them a fight."

"But why didn't you want a funeral home here, it surely would be better than these vacant homes?" I thought as I thanked him for the information and quickly drove off without revealing any of my intentions.

My mind kept wandering back to those two homes. The land was located near good shopping, was fairly flat and was deep enough to put in a cul-de-sac. I soon ordered a plat plan from the city.

The next step was to find out if the McGilleys would sell and what their price was. I didn't waste any time setting up an appointment with the two McGilley boys. "Yes" they would sell. They had spent so much time and money trying to get the land zoned that they were ready to get rid of it. "Make us an offer," one of them blurted out. However, they finally decided that they would sell to me for what they had paid six years earlier. I agreed to the price subject to financing and zoning. I wrote up the contract with only a thousand dollars' earnest money, and to my surprise they signed.

I drove home that afternoon thanking God that I had been able to tie up the land for a year with only a thousand dollars down. That would surely please Charles. To celebrate I rushed to McGonigle's meat market to pick up some loin lamb chops, Charles' favorite meal.

After dinner I decided to tell Charles what I had done. "I'm not surprised, dear. However, I'm afraid you might have a bigger project on your hands than you think."

"If I don't try, I'll never know," was my immediate response. Charles smiled in agreement.

The next morning I called my architect, Howard Nearing.

Luckily, he was in and had time to see me. I showed him the plat plan and explained my ideas. When he questioned the location on a busy corner, I defended my case by assuring him that the six-foot wall surrounded by trees would keep out the noise. After further discussion, Howard agreed to design the layout.

I immediately ordered a topography map of the land and Howard proceeded to design a cul-de-sac, including twelve home sites. I hired an artist to draw a picture in water color to depict my ideas. The artist did a great job, capturing my ideas to perfection.

Next, came the job of getting the bids on utilities, street, wall, gates, and so on. I spent days searching for the best contractors. The engineer I hired was very helpful, and within weeks I had my budget ready. I would need $500,000, including the cost of the land.

Since Charles and I had done business with the United Missouri Bank for years, I made an appointment to see the vice president of the bank. With picture (24"x 28") in hand I was ushered into his office. After attentively listening to my ideas, his quick response was, "Mary, it sounds like a great idea but I'm afraid the bank isn't interested at this time in lending money on residential development." I thanked him for his time, picked up my picture and left.

As I walked out of the bank, I looked across the street to the First National Bank. I didn't have an appointment but why not try, I thought. I did know an officer there. Maybe he would be in. "Is Mr. Wornall in?" I asked the receptionist, who immediately called him on the phone and announced that he had a visitor.

Mr. Wornall's reaction to my idea was the reverse of what I had encountered at the United Missouri Bank. He thought the idea was great and wanted to present it to the board when they met the following Thursday. Friday I got a call saying the bank would lend me $500,000. I was so excited!

I called the McGilley brothers at once to inform them that my financing was in place. Now all I had to do was get the land zoned. I felt sure that the neighbors would love my idea, as it surely was better than the two dilapidated homes sitting on the land.

What a surprise awaited me when I presented the idea to the first neighbor. The woman was hostile and immediately announced that she and the Homes Association would fight my plan. She also reminded me that her husband was a lawyer, who represented the Homes Association. Rushing me to the door, she added that I had better forget the whole idea as the Homes Association would never allow anything more than two homes to be built on that comer.

Surely the other neighbors wouldn't be that rude, I comforted myself. I decided to call the president of the Homes Association, who sounded very friendly and suggested that I present my plan at their next meeting, which would be three weeks later.

It was summer time. The meeting was held in the president's backyard where a tasty picnic lunch was served. About forty people attended. The lady who had been so rude to me earlier was among them, spreading her venom. During the lunch everybody avoided me. After the lunch the president asked me to present my plan and then politely dismissed me.

The neighbors turned it down. It was hard for me to understand why they didn't like the plan, as I knew it would enhance the corner and increase the value of the surrounding homes.

Nevertheless the zoning was scheduled. To present my case I hired Dr. Robert Fielick, who was well experienced in land planning, a Yale graduate and the lawyer who helped write the covenants for the city.

The day of the zoning I went early to the court house where Dr. Fielick was waiting for me. He tried to comfort me by assuring me that I had a good chance to win. People were swarming in, along with newspaper reporters and photographers.

Dr. Fielick presented our side first. In a very professional manner, he explained why we chose to go with the Housing and Urban Development (HUD) plan since it allows the developer the freedom to put up the wall and secure the project with security gates. When I showed the colored picture of the area, the members of the City Council were delighted with the idea.

But when the neighbors' lawyer took the stand, I realized I had a fight on my hands. The neighbors definitely did not want a HUD plan because they feared it would give me too much freedom. Seeing the need for a change in plans, Dr. Fielick asked for a break. In a back room he suggested that we drop the HUD plan and change to a community plan with variances. I agreed, and Dr. Fielick returned to the court room to announce that the developer would drop the HUD plan and change to a community plan with variances. The neighborhood's lawyer was stunned as the zoning committee went on to approve my plan.

I lost no time and proceeded to build Chartwell. I contacted several good builders and sold them all the lots except for two, which I kept for myself. This enabled me to pay off my bank loan much earlier than the bank expected.

Chartwell was off the ground. The builders got started right away and the homes sold quickly. Since my own home was one of the first to be built, I was the first to occupy Chartwell. This was great, as it enabled me to supervise the area while it was being built.

Chartwell turned out to be a landmark in Kansas City. It was the first walled-in, secured residential area in the city.

But I didn't stop there. I had my eye on a piece of land on the Plaza owned by Stan Durwood. Over a ten-year span I called him many times to ask about the land, but his answer was always the same, "Mary, thanks for calling, but I'm not ready to do anything at this time."

One day when I arrived home, my maid gave me the message that I was to call Mr. Durwood. Quite excited, I rushed to return his call. Mr. Durwood asked if he could come out to see Chartwell. "We set up an appointment for two days later. He seemed very pleased with Chartwell and suggested that I do his piece of land on the Plaza – approximately five acres on a hillside over looking the Plaza. What an opportunity!

I immediately called Howard Nearing, my architect, and we got started right away to develop the tract of land. Stan

Durwood approved the plan and gave us the go-ahead. I was off and running! The layout consisted of nine homes to be entered from Sunset Drive and one entering from Ward Parkway. The lots sold quickly because of the location. Another landmark was emerging in Kansas City with my stamp on it.

Next, I eyed a piece of land in Leawood. The owners agreed to sell me five of the ten acres. Their own home was located on the remaining acres, which they wanted to keep. I developed another Chartwell and called it Chartwell West. In all my projects I always gave a lot of thought to the area and made sure that the homes were carefully designed and well built and that the surroundings were beautifully landscaped.

I stuck with my idea of developing a secured residential area and got to develop several other areas like it. I am flattered when I see similar developments built by other developers.

WHEN YOU HAVE A GREAT IDEA, STICK WITH IT.

ALWAYS READY FOR NEW ADVENTURES

After developing Chartwell West there was a lull in my professional life. But it didn't last long. My friend Kip called to have lunch one day. Kip was the top salesman of a large real-estate company in town. He was a very urbane gentleman, always dressed to perfection and driving the latest Lincoln Continental. Best of all, he was very knowledgeable about real estate. We first met when he made a point of meeting me at one of the homes I was previewing. I cooperated frequently with his company and sold a lot of his listings so he had become curious about this Mary Overfelt and how she got all these top executives coming to town. Evidently, we impressed each other and from then on were good friends.

Kip had been offered a vice presidency of Eugene Brown Real Estate Company and now insisted that I join him to manage their new office on College Boulevard. A few years earlier Kip had also recruited me to join him at the Paul Hamilton Company as vice president. But I quickly learned that management was not my cup of tea. I liked to be in the field helping people find that perfect home. So after a short time I returned to my own company. However, I couldn't say no to Kip this time either. What a challenge!

We started the office with two sales ladies. It took a few days to find the right furniture and get the office looking like a well-managed organization. I recruited some good salespeople and we were soon an established office making money for Eugene Brown Real Estate Company. I learned to deal with twenty or more personalities and keep the office running smoothly. However, as at the Paul Hamilton Company I missed working with families and developing new projects.

After a year and a half with Eugene Brown, I received a call from Mr. Harry Lloyd, who wanted me to help develop a piece of land he owned at 168th and Holmes Road. I met with him on a beautiful spring day to review the land. My adrenal glands went crazy as I viewed the rolling land with lots of mature trees.

I wanted to accept the job, but there was a problem. I had a contract with Mr. Brown that had eight more months to go. Mr. Lloyd said he would talk to Mr. Brown and call me the next day. When I reminded him that I was leaving for Acapulco early in the morning, he asked for my phone number there.

Late the next night I got a call from Mr. Lloyd saying I now worked for him. He had bought my contract from Mr. Brown. I knew it was a good opportunity for me, but I had regrets because I enjoyed working for Mr. Brown and I would miss Kip.

Loch Lloyd was then in its elementary stage. The front nine holes of the golf course and the main streets were finished, but the beautiful entrance still lacked security gates.

My work was spelled out for me. The first thing was to get a place for a sales office. Until the clubhouse was built, we used a trailer. We added a deck onto the back of the trailer with double doors so clients could look out on the first fairway and a more attractive entrance.

Those early days were fun and challenging. Mr. Lloyd was anxious to introduce people to his new project. So, before the clubhouse was finished we used a large tent for parties with catered food and live music. Many days I worked late into the night and enjoyed it all.

After I had worked at Loch Lloyd for many months, it became obvious that most of the clientele were people who wanted to size down rather than those wanted to build bigger homes. The lots were large, and in the price bracket that discouraged the budget for small homes. But it didn't take me long to solve that problem.

I had my eye on a small area, approximately five acres, well treed and, in my mind, a perfect spot to build a cluster of smaller homes. After laying out the potential of my idea, and a budget for the project, I presented the idea to Harry Lloyd. To my surprise Harry was very negative about spending his money to develop it. But I was not giving up and asked instead if I could develop it. Harry leaned back in his chair in deep concentration. After a moment he said, "I'll tell you what I'll do. I'll sell you the land." "How much?" Harry quoted me a fair price. I was so excited that I jumped to my feet and said, "Let's shake on that." And we did.

I then immediately phoned to set up an appointment with my banker. Based on my past experience developing other successful areas, I was able to borrow the construction money. Again I got Howard Nearing to help lay out several plans. I decided on one that created a large cul-de-sac with extra parking spaces for the twelve surrounding home sites.

The lots sold quickly. As with Chartwell I chose a lot for my own home. The finished project turned out to be one of the most attractive cul-de-sacs in Loch Lloyd, which pleased Harry, who asked me to supervise other areas like it.

THE SUCCESS OF "THE VILLAGES" AT LOCH LLOYD GAVE ME A FEELING OF STRENGTH. I HAD FOUGHT FOR SOMETHING I BELIEVED IN AND WORKED VERY HARD TO MAKE IT PROSPER.

REFLECTIONS

In the last forty-seven years, selling real estate and developing land has changed drastically. In the past most people bought a home for a lifetime. Now it is not uncommon to buy and sell every five to ten years. Contracts have gotten more detailed as buyers have gotten more sophisticated.

The biggest change I have observed has been in home construction. In the past, depending on the size of the home, it would take at least a year to build. Now homes are being built within four to six months. The vast construction boom taking place has led to a shortage of qualified laborers. There is no time for craftsmanship and less craftsmen are available. Whatever happened to apprenticeship?

Yet with all the pluses and minuses in the selling and developing of land, I must confess that I loved it all. As I look back on my life I found two things I am very good at: overcoming obstacles and rolling with the punches. My courage and determination helped a lot, but I must also give credit to the Man upstairs. Since I was a child I learned to rely on God who has blessed my life.

In the beginning my main purpose was to make enough money to take a trip to Oberammergau. I made that trip and many more. Two African safaris, as well as tours of the east coast of Africa from Tanzania to Cape of Good Hope, Nepal, India, England, Wales, Ireland, Scotland, France, Italy, Germany and many Caribbean islands. All the risks and hard work have paid off.

Proceeds from the sale of this book will be donated to charity.